THIS Picture Knight BOOK
BELONGS TO

....

The Adventures of Maurice Mini Minor

GEOFFREY BAKER

Maurice
cleans up

illustrated by Rolf Harris

**Picture
Knight**

HODDER AND STOUGHTON

For Hazel, Duncan and Geoffrey

From an original idea by Dr P. Mansfield and Terry Moule

British Library Cataloguing in Publication Data

Baker, Geoffrey
Maurice cleans up.
I. Title   II. Harris, Rolf, *1930-*   III. Series
823'.914 [J]

ISBN 0-340-52956-3

First published 1990 by Picture Knight

Published by Hodder and Stoughton Children's Books,
a division of Hodder and Stoughton Ltd,
Mill Road, Dunton Green, Sevenoaks, Kent TN13 2YA
Editorial office: 47 Bedford Square, London WC1E 7DP

Printed in Great Britain by Cambus Litho, East Kilbride

'Here we are,' called Maurice Mini Minor, 'Mr Lovely's Excellent Car Wash and I can't wait.'

'Here, here,' boomed Sir Reginald Hoy-Titoyty, 'the sooner I can smarten up the better. I look as if I've reversed through a hedge.'

Maurice looked at all the dirt that had splattered and splashed onto Sir Reginald's body-work. 'You certainly do,' he said, 'I don't think I've ever seen you looking so splattered and sploshed.'

It had been raining for a whole week and no one could stay clean with so much mud splashing everywhere.

'I think I'm even dirtier than you,' said Maurice who enjoyed driving through as many deep puddles as he could.

'Little cars always look scruffy especially in wet weather,' said Sir Reginald.

Maurice ignored this remark as they drove across to the Car Wash which was billowing with spray and soap and bubbles. Suddenly they saw a very big bubble float out from it and two tiny headlights turn towards them.

'They're attacking,' boomed Sir Reginald, 'take cover.'

'Don't be silly,' said Maurice, 'it's only little Bubbles.'

And so it was. 'That feels better,' she was saying, 'now I can see again. Hallo, Maurice and Sir Reginald, are you going to have a wash too? Can I watch?'

'You first, Maurice,' said Sir Reginald who felt a little foolish now that he realised that he wasn't being attacked by a bubble.

'Right,' said Maurice, putting his money in the machine, 'just hot water for me and then a cold shower at the end. There's nothing quite like it to make you feel full of the joys of your springs.'

In he went. Down came the soft, whirling brushes and a delicious spray of warm water. 'Sizzling steering wheels,' he shrieked, 'it's wonderful and it's marvellous and it tickles!'

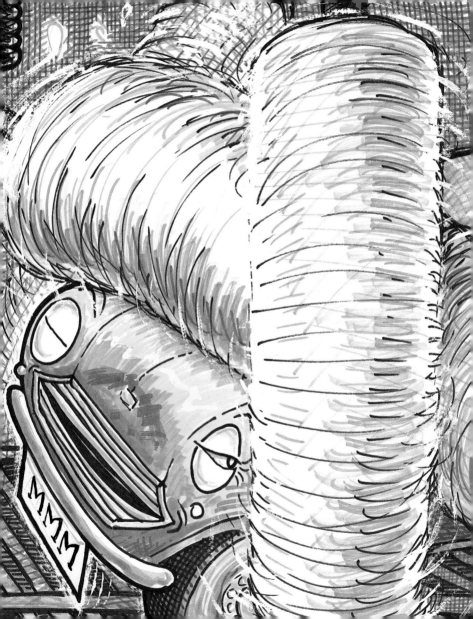

When the brushes stopped whirling, Maurice leaped out giggling. Bubbles got the giggles too, remembering what it was like being tickled all over.

'Now it's my turn,' boomed Sir Reginald, 'and I'm not just having water. I'm having detergent and soap and wax and hot water and two lots at the same time.'

'You can't,' yelled Maurice and Bubbles together.

'Money no object,' boomed Sir Reginald, putting twice as much money as he should into the machine. 'Just you watch this.'

With so much money in it, the Car Wash began to make a rumbly-tummy sort of noise and then it made a *grumbly*-tummy sort of noise and then with a fizz and a pop and a bang, everything burst out of it all at once. There was wax and soap and steam flying everywhere and you should have seen the bubbles as the brushes whirled around much too fast.

Maurice and Bubbles stared in amazement. 'Let me out,' they could hear Sir Reginald shouting. 'Sound the retreat; help!'

Suddenly everything stopped and Sir Reginald appeared. Maurice and Bubbles were trying very, very hard not to laugh. Sir Reginald was covered from roof to wheels in bubbling foam and thick, sticky wax. He looked just like a melted candle.

'Where do you light him?' joked Cheeky Beetle who just happened to be passing.

'Thunder and lightning,' boomed Sir Reginald, 'all my oily parts have gone squeaky and stiff. I'm going to get The Rust, I know I am. I can feel it in my pipes. Thunder and lightning.'

'You'll have to have another wash,' said Maurice, 'and remember this time that all you ever need is warm water and only a tiny bit of soap so that you don't wash all the oil out of you, and then a nice cold shower at the end to make you feel really alive.'

'Hmpf . . . well . . . I'll take your word for it, young man,' muttered Sir Reginald.
'I must remember that too,' giggled Bubbles.

And whilst Sir Reginald went for another simpler wash, Maurice sang a song as he and Bubbles danced around Mr Lovely's Excellent Car Wash.

Remember Sir Reginald, poor old Sir Reg,
Who is better now we hope, all of his
Loverly oil it was washed away
When he went berserk with the soap.
He just went mad with the soap
Yes, he really went mad with the soap.

He thought when he went to the Car Wash
He could afford to pay double
Then he would beam and glow and gleam
Like a beautiful, shining bubble.
But his oil washed away with the soap and
  the spray
Leaving him wracked with pain
He thundered, 'I must beware of the rust
And never use so much soap again.'

Ge-splattered, ge-splottered, ge-splittered,
    ge-spluttered,
Ge-splodged from time to time
If you're ge-splidge-spludge-splodged
From head to toe with gungey grime
You *need* soap when you're grimy
Just a little bit when you're not,
But clean water is best for you
Ge-split, ge-splat, ge-splot.
Yes, clean water is best for you
Ge-split, ge-splat, ge-splot.

I sing this song as I drive along,
Maurice Mini Minor;
I get there soon 'cause I keep in tune,
Maurice Mini Minor;
And when you see me passing by,
Just toot your horn and wink your eye,
No need to wonder who am I,
Maurice Mini Minor.